For my mom, Leslie

I'd like to give a HUGE thank-you to everyone who has listened to me talk about this story over the past almost-decade. Thank you to my family for their constant love and support, thank you to all of my friends for their never-ending encouragement, and thank you to everyone at Random House for all of their faith in my work! Without any of this, Slug would not be here today. I love you all. —JJK

THIS IS A BORZOI BOOK PUBLISHED BY ALFRED A. KNOPF

This is a work of fiction. Names, characters, places, and incidents either are the product of the author's imagination or are used fictitiously. Any resemblance to actual persons, living or dead, events, or locales is entirely coincidental.

Copyright © 2006 by Jarrett J. Krosoczka

All rights reserved. Published in the United States by Alfred A. Knopf, an imprint of Random House Children's Books, a division of Random House, Inc., New York.

KNOPF, BORZOI BOOKS, and the colophon are registered trademarks of Random House, Inc.

www.randomhouse.com/kids

Educators and librarians, for a variety of teaching tools, visit us at www.randomhouse.com/teachers

Library of Congress Cataloging-in-Publication Data
Krosoczka, Jarrett.
My buddy, Slug / Jarrett J. Krosoczka. – 1st ed.
p.   cm.
SUMMARY: When Alex hurts his best friend's feelings, he learns that sometimes staying friends means apologizing.
ISBN-13: 978-0-375-83342-7 (trade) – ISBN-13: 978-0-375-93342-4 (lib. bdg.)
ISBN-10: 0-375-83342-0 (trade) – ISBN-10: 0-375-93342-5 (lib. bdg.)
[1. Best friends–Fiction. 2. Friendship–Fiction. 3. Apologizing–Fiction.] I. Title.
PZ7.K935My 2006   [E]–dc22   2005035613

The illustrations in this book were created using acrylics.

MANUFACTURED IN CHINA
10 9 8 7 6 5 4 3 2 1

First Edition

My Buddy, Slug

Jarrett J. Krosoczka

Alfred A. Knopf ❧ New York

It used to be Slug, Kevin, and me—the unstoppable three. Until Kevin moved away.

Now it's just Slug and me . . .
all the time.

He was everywhere I was . . .

morning,

noon,

and night.

I tried to get some alone time.

At the game . . .

At the library . . .

At the mall . . .

At the dentist . . .

At art class . . .

By faking sick.

It was beginning to be a bit too much.

One day, after a long afternoon, I came home for dinner and my mom called out from the other room, "Honey, we have a guest. . . ."

"More mashed potatoes, Slug?"

"Alex honey," my mother said, "wouldn't it be great if Slug slept over tonight?"

Slug smiled.

I didn't.

We made popcorn
and watched movies.

"OOOoooh! This is my favorite part! This is where that guy comes in and surprises the kids and tells them that there is no treasure. But in the end, he was only telling a lie and there was a treasure, but the kids find out there is anyhow, because there's this magic chipmunk who . . ."

Slug even slept in my bed while
I slept on the floor. Mom said,
"He's your guest."

"Alex. Hey, pssst, Alex. Let's tell scary stories—I'll start."

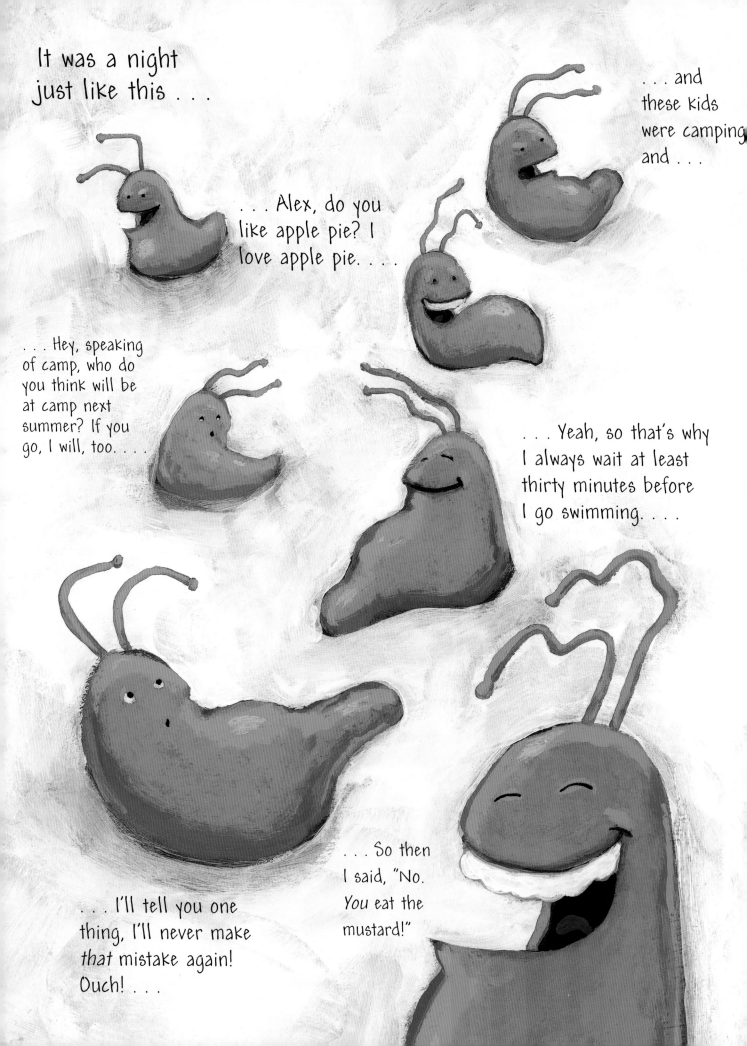

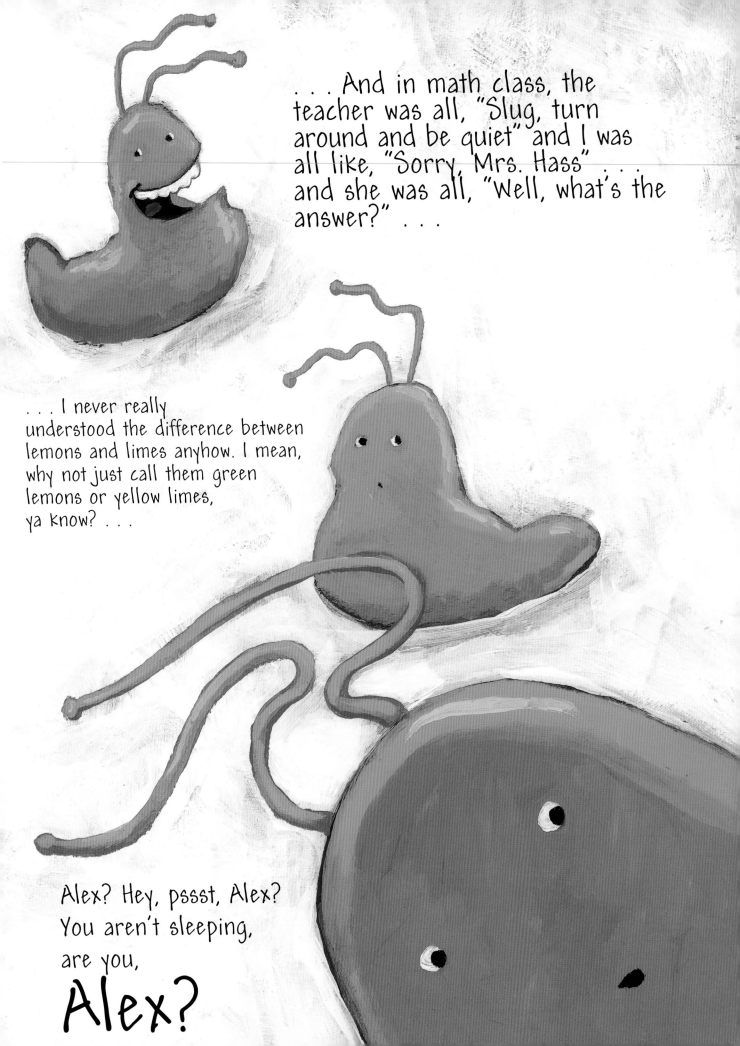

The next morning, I had words
with my mother.

"Why did you invite Slug over?!"
I asked.

She looked surprised. "Well, you're such
good friends and he's so sweet. . . ."

"SWEET?! SWEET?! He's
ANNOYING! And FRIENDS?! . . .
I'M SICK OF HIM!"

I looked to see that Slug had
overheard everything I just said.

"I'll be leaving now.
Thank you."

I didn't see Slug around much afterward.

Kevin was gone
and now so was Slug.

The next week at recess,
Slug was playing basketball.

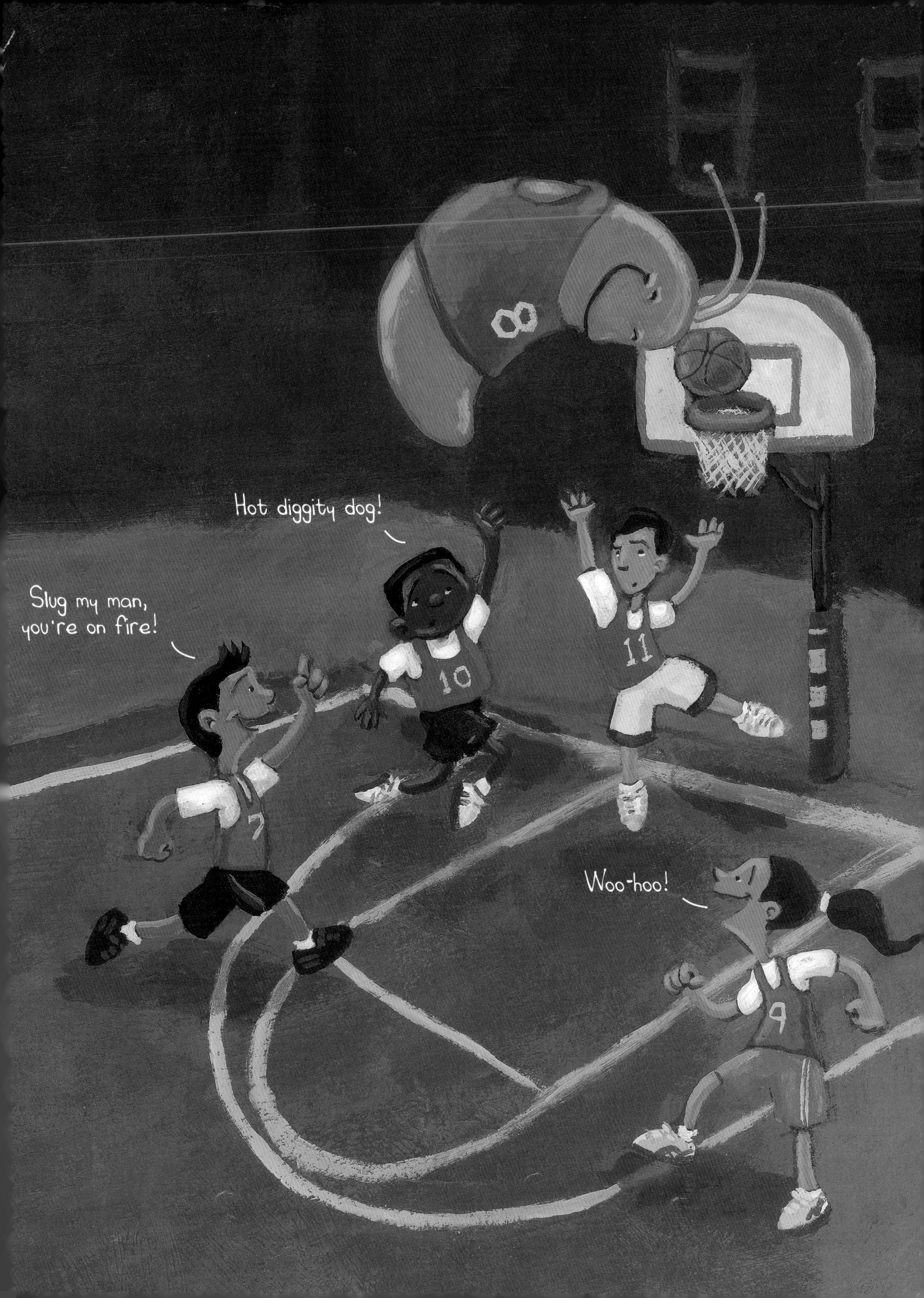
Slug my man, you're on fire!
Hot diggity dog!
Woo-hoo!

When the game was over,
I talked to Slug.

"Uh . . . hey, Slug." Saying
sorry is never easy. "I'm
sorry for saying those mean
things."

"Mmmm-hmmm," said Slug.

"It's just that, you know, we
were with each other all the
time and . . . I guess I just
needed time to hang out on
my own. . . . I didn't mean
to hurt your feelings. . . .
I'm sorry."

"How sorry?"
he asked.

"Really sorry,"
I said.

"Really, really sorry?"
he asked.

"Really, really, really sorry!"
I said.

"Good! Because I've missed you so much! And I guess I was just afraid that you would, like, move away, too, like Kevin did, or something. . . . But I'm glad we're friends again! I've been dying to tell you about this new detective kit I got. Well, it's more of a spy kit and it has a secret decoder ring and binoculars and the other day I was using it to spy on my neighbor who was working in her garden and she was all, 'Scram, you crazy Slug!' And I was all like, 'Ahhh!' and I ran back to my house and then . . ."